MAGIC STARS

MAGIC SLATE

Magic Stars

Grey Wolf Book 1

Ilona Andrews

Magic Stars
Copyright © 2015 by Ilona Andrews
ISBN: 9781519762337

NYLA Publishing
350 7th Avenue, Suite 2003, NY 10001, New York.
http://www.nyliterary.com

CHAPTER ONE

D erek moved fast on quiet feet.

The bartender downstairs, a stocky woman with hard eyes and a harder jaw, hadn't heard him. She just happened to look up as he made his way to the staircase leading to the back rooms. She reached for the shotgun she kept under the bar, then saw his face and changed her mind. The face used to be a problem, but he'd grown used to it. He knew his eyes assured people that the inside matched the outside, and so the bartender turned away and let him walk up the stairs. It was an old wooden staircase, probably pre-Shift, before the magic waves had battered the world and its technological marvels to dust. It must've creaked and sung under the weight of humans every day, but the worn steps kept their peace this time. He knew where to put his feet.

A short hallway stretched before him, two doors on the right, three doors on the left. Unlit. The owner was trying to save on electricity or the charged-air bill. The rooms were empty, all but one, the second on the left. He paused by the door and listened. On the other side of an inch-thick piece of wood people talked and moved. Five. All men, drinking and talking in low voices. The draft from under the door brought the odor of cheap beer to his nostrils mixed with the metallic stench of human blood. He'd followed this scent across half the city.

People lied. Scents never did.

The shadows under the door indicated a single light source. The magic was down. The light leaking through the crack under the door was electric, buttery yellow, and judging by the hallway, the owner was too cheap to spring for anything but a single lightbulb. He reached into the pocket of his jeans with his left hand and pulled out a rock he'd picked up outside. This didn't warrant the claws. He took a knife out of its sheath. It was a simple combat knife, fixed blade seven inches long, coated in black epoxy, so it didn't catch the light.

The five men inside heard nothing, their voices still calm. Relaxed.

Derek thought back to the house from which he'd come, leaned back, and kicked the door. It splintered, bursting open under the impact of his superhuman strength, and he hurled the rock at the lonely light fixture above the table. Glass shattered, and the room plunged into darkness.

His instincts punched a cocktail of hormones into his bloodstream in an electric rush. Darkness blossomed, opening up like a flower, revealing five heartbeats wrapped in scent. His mind signaled "prey," propelling him through the darkness toward the first warm body scrambling to pull a gun. Derek sliced across the man's throat. The knife sank deep, too deep, severing bone. Overkill. He was a little too excited. He spun to the left, dodging a bullet before he saw the starburst of the muzzle flash across the room, grabbed the man in his way, and punched the knife into his chest. The heart ruptured. Derek jerked his knife out and spun away to crouch by the wall.

Shots popped, loud in the small room. They were firing blind, panicking.

A heartbeat straight across from him, the man spinning wildly, his gun spitting bullets.

Boom, boom, boom . . . click.

He cleared the table between them in a single leap, the impact of his weight knocking the man off his feet. He landed on top of the gunman and severed the carotid and jugular with one fast, precise stroke. The fourth man spun and fired in the direction of the noise, but Derek was already moving, leaping forward in a crouch. He knocked the shooter's arm aside, sank his knife into the man's groin, twisted, and dragged it up. The man screamed and went down.

Two heartbeats gone, two rapidly fading, one fast and frantic. Someone in the room was still alive. His nostrils flared. The odor of blood swirled around him, intoxicating, demanding more. More blood; more murder; more living, kicking prey struggling in his fingers; more fresh meat he could bite and rip. He shut the bloodlust off, put the knife on the table, and paused to pinpoint the faint sound of a human being trying to breathe quietly through his mouth. *There.* He stalked across the room, avoiding puddles of blood cooling on the floor. The man lay flat, hugging the floor. Derek crouched in one fluid motion, locked his hand on the man's throat, and dragged him up. The man gurgled, writhing in his hand, trying to claw with feeble nails at the arm that held him. One squeeze, one crunch of bones, and it would be over.

Derek dragged him to the back of the room and jerked the thick curtain open. Moonlight spilled onto his captive, enameling his tortured face with blue. White, short dark hair, at least thirty, old enough to know what he had done. A professional criminal.

Derek grabbed a chair with his other hand, set it against the window, and slammed the man into it. The thug sagged, desperately trying to suck some air into his lungs. His eyes widened, his pupils so large with fear, their blackness swallowed the irises, leaving only a narrow ring of blue.

"I know you," the thug squeezed out, his voice hoarse. "You're Derek Gaunt."

Good. This would go faster. "Six hours ago, the five of you broke into the home of Randall and Melissa Ives."

"They weren't shapeshifters, I swear. I swear they weren't."

"You put two shots into Randall in the hallway and left him to bleed out. You killed Melissa in the kitchen, three shots, two to the head, one to the chest."

The man's eyes bulged.

"Then you went upstairs and shot ten-year-old Lucy Ives and her seven-year-old brother Michael. You annihilated the whole family. The question is why?"

"They weren't shapeshifters!"

"No, they were human beings. They were also smiths." Derek reached over and took the knife from the table. "Melissa Ives made this knife."

He thrust the knife into the man's stomach and cut a long shallow line from one hip to the other. Blood gushed from the cut. The air smelled sour as the blade slashed the intestines. The man let out a ragged yowl of pain and choked on his own terror.

"Why?" Derek asked.

"They had a rock." The man squeezed the words between sharp gasps. "Some kind of metal rock. Caleb wanted it."

"Caleb Adams?"

The man nodded, trembling. "Yes. Him."

Caleb Adams had started out as a witch, but his coven had cast him out. He'd proclaimed himself a warlock, and now he ran a gang on the edge of the Warren. Bordered by South-View Cemetery and Lakewood Park, the Warren had begun as part of the urban renewal project, but magic had hit it hard. It was poor, treacherous, and vicious, a war zone where gangs battled with each other. Caleb Adams felt right at home. He was violent and power-hungry, and according to the latest street talk, he was defending his new turf against two other gangs and losing.

"Where is the rock now?"

"We couldn't find it."

Time for a more detailed conversation. He raised his knife.

"We couldn't find it!" the man cried out. "I swear! We trashed the house looking for it. Rick and Colin shot the guy and his wife, and they both died before we could ask."

"Why did you shoot the children?"

"That was Colin. He shot the woman and then ran straight upstairs. He just went nuts."

He wished he knew which one was Colin. Sadly, he couldn't kill him again.

"What does this rock look like?"

"About the size of a big orange. Shiny metal rock. It glows if you take it outside in the moonlight."

The man's breathing slowed. The bleeding was taking its effect. "Three . . . ," he whispered.

"Three what?"

"Three pieces of a rock. Rick said the rock had broken . . . into three chunks. Rick said Caleb already had one and wanted all three. He sent . . . two crews out. I don't know where the other crew went. I told you . . . everything. Don't kill me."

Derek's lips stretched into a smile on their own, driven not by humor but by the instinctual need to bare his teeth as the wild inside glared through his eyes. "There is gunpowder stench on your hand and blood spatter on your shirt. It smells like Michael Ives."

The man froze.

Derek smiled wider. "I don't make deals with child murderers."

The night was blue.

The deep sky breathed, as if alive, the small glowing dots of distant stars winking at him as he ran along the night streets. The moon had rolled out and soared, huge and round, spilling a cascade of liquid silver onto the half-ruined city. It called to him the way it called to all wolves. If he didn't have a job to do, he would've run right out of Atlanta into the magic-fed forest beyond, abandoned his human skin for fur and four paws, and sang to it. His human vocal cords had sustained too much damage in the same fight that had altered his face, but his wolf voice was as good as always. He would soak in that silver glow until it shone from his eyes and sing a long song about hunting and running through the dark wood in the middle of the night. On nights like these he remembered that he was only twenty. But he had someplace to be.

Caleb's five killers hadn't gone too far from the house they destroyed, barely five miles, so he dropped into an easy run, a four-minute mile at best, and let the night air expand his lungs. The Casino flashed by, a white castle turned green by moonlight. He could just make out the gaunt, inhuman shapes of vampires crawling along its parapets, each undead telepathically driven by a human navigator. He made it a point to kill them when the opportunity presented itself.

It didn't come up too often—vampires belonged to the People, and the People and Kate had an uneasy truce. He didn't agree with it, but it was necessary. Sometimes you had to put your personal feelings aside and do what was necessary.

A magic wave flooded the world, snuffing out the rare electric lights, and ignited the charged air within the twisted glass tubes of fey lanterns. The magic-fed light was blue and eerie. Power filled him. His muscles turned stronger; his heart pumped more blood with each beat; the scents and sounds sharpened. It was like walking through the world with a translucent plastic hood covering your head and having it suddenly ripped off. The air tasted fresh. Pure joy filled him, and for a brief moment he forgot the slaughtered family, grinned, and just ran.

The right street loomed too soon. He leapt, bounced off an oak to make a sharp turn, and dropped into the deep indigo shadows by a house. His ears caught noises of furniture being knocked around. Someone was rummaging through the Iveses' home. The neighborhood was too nice for looters.

The crashing stopped.

He waited for a long moment.

Nothing.

He was upwind from them. It was possible that they had stopped for their own reasons. It was also possible that they smelled him. Only one way to find out.

Derek straightened and walked toward the house.

Three people walked out of the building and spread out on the street, moving with telltale balance. Shapeshifters. Definitely not one of the Beast Lord's city crews. He knew all of the shapeshifters who worked in the city, and they knew him. These three didn't look familiar. A Pack city crew would have no business being here anyway. The Iveses were human, and the house sat way past the invisible boundary that carved Atlanta into Pack territory and the rest of the city.

The three guys stretched their shoulders. He stayed in the shadows. They probably couldn't see his face clearly, not with the hood up, but they had caught his scent and showed no reaction. They had no idea who he was. That left two possibilities: Either they were intruders into Pack territory, in which case they were suicidally stupid, or they were new to the Pack, probably part of the seven-family pack Jim, the Beast Lord, had formally accepted into the Atlanta Pack last month. And here they were, looting a dead family's house.

Jim would just love that.

All three were young: late teens, early-twenties. A jackal on the left, the tallest of the three, with a loose mop of red hair. A wolf on the right, compact, light brown hair. He hadn't thought he recognized the scent at first, but now that he'd sampled it for a while, the wolf did smell faintly familiar. The guy in the middle had the build of a wrestler. The scent said cat and a large one.

The cat leaned back and raised his chin. Long dark hair, big round eyes. Confident. They were about the same age, and the cat was clearly sizing him up. His eyes said he liked to fight and didn't lose often. There was a first time for everything.

"You're a long way from the Keep," Derek said.

"You stink like blood," the jackal said.

That would be a clue, if you weren't stupid.

"He smells odd." The wolf wrinkled his nose, trying to figure out what was under the blood. "Almost like a loup."

He'd heard that one before. Sometimes memories he kept hidden deep under the last six years broke out, and his body reacted. It was the corpse of Lucy Ives that had done it. He'd found his youngest sister just like that, curled into a ball in her own blood. She'd been ten, too.

"He isn't a loup," the cat said. "Loups can't stay human. But he isn't Pack. If he was, you'd know him. Which means he's got no business hanging around here."

"Walk away," Derek said.

"What?" The cat squinted. "I can't hear you, outsider. Maybe we should show him what the Pack does to trespassers."

They were too stupid or too new to know that official Pack policy dictated that uninvited guests were to be politely but firmly directed to visit the Keep or clear out of their territory in three days. The Pack didn't threaten or intimidate. They didn't need to. It was a lesson this dumbass would learn quickly. Pain was an excellent teacher.

The Pack had become the largest shapeshifter organization in the country, with the exception of Alaska's Ice Fury, and it claimed a vast territory, covering the entire states of Georgia and North Carolina, and stretching down to Florida. Unaffiliated shapeshifters weren't permitted within the Pack borders. They had three days to present themselves to Pack authority and petition for admission to the Pack or be asked to leave. The Pack was strong and many wanted to join, but absorbing the newcomers and settling them into the existing power structure took time. Back when Curran was the Beast Lord and Kate was his Consort, Curran had capped the admission to the Pack. Jim, the current Beast Lord, followed that policy. He didn't want the Pack to grow too fast, especially not now, since the title of the Beast Lord had changed hands only months ago and his hold on power was still tenuous. For some reason, this particular small pack had been allowed to join. Right now Derek couldn't see why.

A loud clopping of hooves made them all turn. A rider emerged from the side street. You noticed the horse first. You couldn't help it. Built like a small draft horse, with powerful hindquarters and a solid body, she had a muscular neck and the stupid hair on the shins that made it hard to see where her hooves were when she kicked you, which she'd tried to do the first time she'd smelled him. The horse itself was black, or rather almost black, spotted with very faint grey dapples, but the leg hair—feathers, he remembered, although why the hell they called it feathers made no sense to him—was white. The mane was white too, ridiculously long, and wavy. It was wavy because the horse's owner braided it and sometimes put flowers into it. Because she couldn't get a normal horse. She had to have a draft version of My Little Pony.

"What the hell kind of horse is that?" the jackal asked.

"Gypsy horse." He couldn't keep the distaste out of his voice. That and the Friesian were the only two horse breeds he recognized, because he had had no choice about learning them.

The Gypsy horse moved into the moonlight, carrying her rider without any effort, which wasn't much of an accomplishment, since the rider was sixteen years old, barely five-and-a-half feet tall, and weighed maybe a hundred and twenty pounds. If she was soaking wet and wearing all her clothes and carrying both of her tomahawks.

He opened his mouth and closed it. Julie was wearing a bluish T-shirt with the words *Wild Magic* stitched on it and a pair of jean shorts. Her long bare legs stood out against the horse's black hide. Her blonde hair was pulled back into a ponytail, leaving her long neck exposed. A neck that would be frighteningly easy to snap even for a normal human.

The cat was checking her out. She was a kid. He was looking at her like she was dessert. Nothing good was going through his head.

Derek bit off the words, fighting a snarl. "What the fuck are you looking at?"

The cat grinned, baring his teeth. "Bonus."

So that was the cat's plan: Kill him and get Julie. Good plan. If Derek had both hands tied behind his back and his feet chained to the ground.

Julie waved at him and winked at the three shapeshifters. "You shouldn't corner Big Bad Wolves like him on a dark street. It's bad for your health."

"What the hell are you doing here?" he growled. She shouldn't be here. Not in the middle of the night and not in front of this house. He didn't want to tell her what had happened in the house.

"I'm working," she said.

"Why are you dressed like that?"

Her eyes narrowed. "Dressed like what?"

"That."

"There is nothing wrong with the way she's dressed." The cat smirked, flashing white teeth. "I like it."

Laugh it up while you can. "Shut up. If I decide to ask for your opinion, I'll say, 'Hey dickhead,' so you don't get confused."

The cat snarled back. "What the hell makes you think you can tell me what to do?"

Julie sighed. "Look, I don't have time for one of your man things, where you stand around and insult each other. The city has a Guardian, and I'm her Herald. I have a task, and you're between me and my destination. Clear your asses out of here or be destroyed."

"What the actual fuck is going on here?" the jackal asked.

That was about enough of it. Derek stepped forward, moving out of the shadows into the moonlight.

The cat's eyebrows crept up. "What the hell happened to your face?"

"Oh shit." The wolf raised his hands, backed away, and sat down on the ground. "I submit. I meant no offense. Tell Curran I meant no offense."

The cat and the jackal stared at him.

"What's your problem?" the jackal asked.

"That's the Beast Lord's Wolf." The wolf raised his hands palms out. "And that's the Beast Lord's daughter. I'm out."

"I've seen the Beast Lord," the cat said. "He's black, his mate is Asian, and they don't have kids."

"Not that Beast Lord, you moron," the wolf said. "The first one. The ex-Beast Lord."

"Wait," the jackal said. "There is another Beast Lord?"

They were idiots. He was about to fight two idiots.

"You can't challenge him," the wolf said.

"The hell I can't." The cat bared his teeth.

"If you fight him, it's to the death," the wolf warned.

"I don't care."

"Toooooooday." Julie drew the word out.

"I'll fucking kill you!" the cat declared. "I'll rip your throat out and feed it to you."

Yes, he'd never heard that one before.

Julie sighed again and glanced at him. "This is taking way too long. That was a declaration of murderous intent. We're clear. The big one is yours; I'll take the ginger."

They moved at the same time. He was a shapeshifter and she was human, so he won the race. But, he reflected, sprinting toward the cat as one of her tomahawks hurtled through the air and sliced into the jackal's chest, the gap between their reaction time was getting uncomfortably short, and not because he was slowing down.

In front of him, the cat's human skin tore. The cascade of pheromones hit Derek, the chemical catastrophe of magic that signaled the change from human to an animal. The cat hopped back, buying time as his body split, bones shooting up, flesh spiraling up the new bigger, thicker limbs, and golden fur sprouted over it, packed with dense dark rosettes. A leopard. That's why all the smirking. A big cat against a wolf was usually a done deal. Especially a big cat who could maintain the warrior form, a meld of beast and human.

The wereleopard landed upright on huge paws, claws out, hulking. Big jaws. At least a hundred and fifty pounds heavier, and that weight was muscle and bone. Stupid stance, though, arms out. Very little or no training. Probably relied on his strength, speed, and size. It wouldn't be enough this time.

He was well within his rights to kill the leopard. Derek belonged to Curran, who had formally retired from the Pack, taking his people with him, which put him outside of Pack structure. He had no position within the Pack's hierarchy. The only thing Derek could be challenged for was his life, and Pack law said he could end his attacker without fear of retribution.

The cat swiped at him. Derek ducked under the slice, but the claws grazed his shoulder in a burning flash of pain. The scent of his own blood lashed him. Fast bastard. Derek carved a long gash across the cat's ribs as he darted under, spun around, and sank a solid kick into the small of the cat's back. The cat's spine crunched. The wereleopard leapt away and spun around, golden eyes glowing.

If he killed the leopard, the relationship between the new-comers and the Pack would be strained. Jim would be pissed. He needed a few seconds to figure out if he gave a damn.

On the left the jackal launched himself into a spectacu-lar jump, aiming for Julie on her horse. He hurtled through the air, eyes wide, mouth open. She tossed a handful of yel-low powder into his face. The reek of wolfsbane streaked through the street. His eyes watered. The jackal collapsed on the ground.

The cat leaped at Derek, going high, claws of his right paw raised for the kill. Once you were airborne, there was no way to change the direction.

Derek let go of the knife, sidestepped to the left, grabbed the cat's right forearm with his right hand as the wereleopard flew by, and drove his left hand into the cat's right thigh, channeling all the power and momentum of the wereleopard's leap into a flip. The cat practically flipped himself. The wereleopard's back slapped the ground. The air burst out of his lungs. Derek dropped down, swiped his knife off the pavement, and buried it in the cat's gut. Sour stench wafted up into his nostrils.

The cat snarled and swiped at him. The big claws tore at his chest, shredding his T-shirt. Derek broke free. The cat jerked up, lighting quick, and turned into a whirlwind of claws. Derek dodged, backing away, noting each graze that stung his shoulders. The leopard chased him, eyes mad, pupils so wide the gold of his irises had shrunk to a thin ring. When the cats snapped like this, there was no fighting them. You had to block what you could until you got some distance.

"I kirrl you!" the cat yowled.

Speaking in warrior form indicated real talent. That's why the small pack had been allowed to join. Jim had plans for the leopard.

A cut. The cat was swinging wildly, his response sharpened by the wound in his stomach. Derek had been like that, too, years ago, until he learned to register the pain without it feeding his anger.

If he killed the cat, Jim would be pissed off, but more importantly, Curran would regret the waste of talent. The Pack still mattered to him, even if he said it didn't.

Another cut stung his left shoulder. The cat had little training but good instincts. The trouble with instincts is that they can be used against you.

Derek rolled down onto his back, bending his knees and bringing up his feet. The leopard lunged at him without thinking, reacting to the falling prey. Derek kicked, ramming his feet into the cat's furry stomach, reopening the freshly sealed gash. The big shapeshifter hurtled over his head. Derek flipped onto his stomach and into a crouch, the movement practiced so many times, he didn't even have to think about it. The cat was scrambling to his feet. He was fast, but nobody had taught him how to fall. It cost him a precious half a second.

You could do a lot with half a second. Derek spun, picking up power, and snapped a roundhouse kick to the leopard's head just as the big cat finally rose. His lower shin connected, the powerful muscles of his thigh delivering hundreds of pounds of force to the leopard's ear and temple. It would've burst the eardrum and cracked the skull of a human, causing an incapacitating concussion.

The leopard swayed, still snarling, his swipes sluggish.

Derek lunged forward, dodged the claws, and smashed the heel of his right hand into the leopard's left shoulder, shoving him back just as he kicked the leopard's calves, sweeping his legs from under him. The big cat crashed down, his head bouncing off the pavement. Derek followed, hammering punches onto the cat's face. One, two, three. He'd broken baseball bats with a punch before.

Five, six.

"You're going to kill him," Julie warned.

"No." *But he won't be smiling at any girls for the next three months.*

"Derek?"

"Yes?" One more.

Suddenly he was aware of her standing next to him. A metal chain dangled in his view.

The cat's body deflated. The fur melted back into human skin. His face looked like raw hamburger. By morning the skin would be back to normal. The broken jaw and the three teeth he'd knocked out would take a couple of months to heal and grow back.

Julie shook the handcuffs at him.

"Fine."

He took the handcuffs, flipped the woozy cat over, pulled his arms over, and locked them on the cat's now-human wrists. The handcuffs were a shapeshifter edition: Each band was lined with silver spikes. Trying to snap the chain by pulling the cuffs apart drove the spikes into the skin. Silver burned like fire. He was sure the cat would stay put.

Derek tilted his head. The jackal lay on his back in a puddle of his own blood, trussed up like a hog, wrists and ankles tied together. The wound on his chest looked deep, but Julie had missed the heart. Knowing her, on purpose. He would heal.

Derek tilted his head and looked at the remaining wolf. He knew his eyes glowed, reflecting the moonlight.

"We were at a bar," the wolf said. "Eli and Nathan are new to the city, so I took them to the Steel Horse. A guy came up to us and asked if we were up for making a quick five hundred bucks."

There was no such thing as a quick $500, especially not in Atlanta after dark.

"He gave us the address of this house. We're supposed to go in and sniff out a rock." The wolf lifted his hands, holding them apart, fingers almost touching. "About this big. Glows in the moonlight. We went into the house and smelled the blood. We were trying to decide what to do when you showed up."

"Four hours ago someone killed the human family who lived in this house for that rock," Derek said. "Husband, wife, two kids."

"I didn't know," the wolf said, his voice pleading. "I swear I didn't know. You've got to believe me."

Julie squinted at the house. "Is that the Iveses' house?"

He'd hoped she wouldn't recognize it, but she had just been there two weeks ago, buying a knife with Kate. He nodded. There was nothing else to do.

Her eyes went wide. "All of them?"

He nodded again.

She clamped her hand over her mouth. He put his arm around her before he knew he'd done it. She stuck her face into his shredded T-shirt.

He hugged her gently and wished he could make it better.

The world was a fucked-up place. A girl like Julie shouldn't know people who had been violently murdered. He shouldn't know them. Instead they met in front of a slaughterhouse. He'd killed five people tonight, and she'd opened a man's chest with her tomahawk.

"What were you supposed to do with the rock?" he asked, still holding Julie.

"Take it to Pillar Rock," the wolf said. "What do you want me to do?"

"Go down this street until you run into Manticore. Turn left, go two blocks. You'll see a white building with a green roof. That's the Pack safe house for this quadrant of the city. Tell them what happened and call your alpha."

"Should I call their alphas, too?" he asked.

"No. Just call Desandra. She'll handle it. Tell her I consider the matter closed." Knowing Desandra, she would enjoy informing the other alphas that their new members had stepped in it.

The wolf exhaled, turned, and sprinted down the street at fifty miles per hour. In ten minutes the pickup team would swarm the area.

Julie pulled away from him. Her eyes were red. She never sobbed when she cried. She used to, but something had happened in the last year, and now she cried like that, without moving or making a sound. It was worse somehow.

"Hey," he said.

"Hey." She wiped her eyes with the back of her hand. "Did you find out who killed the Iveses?"

He nodded again.

"Are they dead?"

"Yes."

"Good," she said, sudden viciousness in her voice. She sidestepped him and went into the house.

He knew this was it, all of the grief she would show. He'd seen her go through things like that before. Julie had spent three years on the street, where people lived by animal rules, and she'd learned them well: Never show a weakness; never show pain. The vulnerable get eaten. She would break down later when she was alone, but neither he nor anyone else would ever see it.

Yellow crime tape was too expensive to produce in the world that hated factories and plastics, and the cops rarely used it anymore. A single white sticker, slapped across the door and frame, barred entry to the house, and the shapeshifters had already cut it. The door stood wide open, and she went inside. He followed her.

Before the Shift, the processing of a murder scene could take days. Now it took three hours, because murders were plentiful and cops were stretched thin. It was all the time they could spare.

Julie walked straight to the built-in bookcase in the living room, took several books off the shelf, picking them up together, and set them on the floor. Behind the books, a single narrow slit indicated a hidden niche. She pried at it with her nails, and a small section of the wall fell forward, revealing a dark opening and a plastic box inside. Julie pulled it out and popped the lid.

They stared at the rock. A little larger than a softball, it resembled pyrite, fool's gold, except it was bluish white and glowed gently with a cold, dispassionate light. Most of it was rounded, but on one side the stone ended sharply, as if a part had broken off. The hair on the back of his neck rose. He couldn't explain why, but something about that rock made him wary. If he were in his wolf form, he would've circled it on careful paws and left it where it lay.

"Do you see anything?"

Julie frowned. Sensates like her saw the magic in an array of colors, something other people tried to duplicate by building m-scanners.

"Pale bluish silver glow."

"Divine?" Divine objects and creatures glowed with silver.

"No, not divine. White and blue. Different kind of white."

"What registers this kind of white?"

"Elemental magic." She looked at him, her eyes bottomless. "They killed the Iveses for *this*?"

"Yes."

She shook her head and peered at the rock. "What are you?"

He half expected the rock to answer, but it stayed silent, glowing weakly.

"What are you doing here?" he asked.

"Someone jumped Luther," she said.

"Luther? The Biohazard wizard?"

"Yep. Kate is out with Curran, so I took the call. They didn't kill him, probably because they knew he worked for Biohazard, and they didn't want a whole gaggle of mages hunting them down, so they hit him over the head as he was stepping out of his car. He doesn't remember it. He remembers parking and then waking up on the ground with a headache and a bloody head. That afternoon someone brought him a rock. They claimed it fell from the sky and glowed under moonlight, and they wanted a thousand dollars for it. The magic was down by the time the rock got to Luther, so he bargained them down to three hundred bucks. He tried to get a sample to analyze, but he couldn't cut it at his lab—nothing worked—so he took it to the Mage College, where they managed to slice a small flake from it. He was bringing the rock back to Biohazard when he was attacked."

She reached into the pocket of her shorts and pulled out a small plastic vial. Inside, a tiny crumb of the rock glowed. "Luther is down with a concussion, so he couldn't go look for it."

And he wouldn't ask his colleagues for help, because they'd ask why the hell he'd taken a possibly magic rock out of the Biohazard building. She probably hadn't told him she would be the one doing the job. Most likely Luther thought Kate was on it. He would've done the same in her place. Why worry the client? As long as the job gets done, it doesn't matter who does it.

"So I went to the place where the rock was found, climbed the building, and waited for the magic to hit." She tapped the container. "The rock's magic shines like a tiny star. If you know what to look for, you can see it from miles away."

Which meant that if Caleb could see it, he would know exactly where they were at all times. "Any way to hide it?"

She shook her head. "It's magic, Derek. I saw it through the house. Your turn. Why are you here?"

He started with a call from Curran and coming to the house where Hope, Melissa Ives' sister, frantically rocked herself, crying hysterically. Curran and Kate patronized that shop. It was a well-known fact, and when she found the bodies, she called 911 first and Curran second. Curran, in turn, had called him. His orders simple: Find the people responsible and make sure they never do it again. How exactly he went about it was up to him. He made sure to have Melissa Ives' sister sign the contract hiring him and Kate and Curran's firm to investigate the murder. Anything he did in the pursuit of the investigation gave him a blanket umbrella of self-defense. After speaking to the overworked detective at the scene, he doubted he'd need it, but Kate liked to keep things legal, and he respected her wishes.

He glossed over finding the bodies. He did tell her about Caleb Adams, the rock that broke in three parts, and the dead men in the bar. Her face got tighter and tighter as he spoke.

"I hate people," she said when he finished.

He wasn't a fan of people either.

"What does it do?" he asked, looking at the rock.

"I don't know."

Whatever it was, people were willing to kill for it. The mission parameters had changed, he decided. He would still punish Adams for killing the Iveses. But he would have to recover the rock as well. It was too dangerous to be left uncontained.

A light noise came from the outside. He inhaled. Patricia, one of Jim's shapeshifter agents; Nicolas; and two others whose scents he knew well. They'd come to pick up the injured. They'd smell him and Julie. If they had any questions, they'd look them up.

Julie tilted her head, giving him an appraising look. "So, Pillar Rock or Caleb Adams?"

She wouldn't let go of this, and he wasn't fool enough to try to convince her otherwise. Once Julie got a case, she was like a wolf with a bone. A dog would give up a treat for his human; a wolf surrendered it to no one. She could see the rock's magic, and he couldn't. He could either work with her and get this done faster and safer, or he could go off on his own. The latter brought no benefits, and he would wonder where she was and what she was doing the entire time.

"Pillar Rock," he said. "We know where Caleb is likely to be. We know we'll have to go and see him at some point tonight."

"Him and his gang of enforcers who think they are big and bad." Julie's eyes narrowed. "We should talk to them about the Iveses."

"We will," he promised. "We don't know who is at Pillar Rock. Maybe it's a third party."

"Maybe it's Caleb." Julie smiled.

"If we're lucky."

They looked at each other. In that moment he knew they were thinking the exact same thing. Caleb Adams didn't know the Ives family, but before the night was over, he would regret their deaths. He would regret them more than he ever regretted anything in his life.

Chapter Two

Pillar Rock thrust out of the ground among the ruins of North DeKalb Mall, a little over five miles away. He could've run it in half an hour, even if he took his time and carried Julie, which would be faster than her horse picking her way through the treacherously degraded streets. But Peanut had to come along and she trotted at about eight miles per hour, so he kept pace with a light jog.

He'd pointed out before that the horse was neither brown nor peanut-shaped, so the name didn't describe her in any way, and he was told that was the point. He let it lie. Some things you simply accepted, the way you accepted the sunrise or the winter cold. They called it lupine fatalism, but in reality it was plain common sense.

The moon lit their way. The north side of the city fought a never-ending battle with encroaching wilderness. On some streets, the pavement had worn away, surrendering to the forest growth, but North Druid Hills Road was still somewhat clear, if overgrown. Here and there a rusty car poked through the spring weeds, pushed or driven off the road just far enough to not block the way. The trees grew thick here, their massive branches shading the road, painting it in patches of shadow and light. Behind them houses crouched, most still occupied. The closer they got to North

DeKalb Mall, the fewer houses would be occupied. The wilderness was frightening now to most humans. They sought safety in numbers, migrating toward the center of the city.

The wilderness never bothered him. He loved it.

He wondered idly if Julie liked it, too. He'd never asked her.

He wondered about many things he never talked about—most of the time there was no need for questions. He would get his answers if he waited long enough. However, she had said something that required a clarification.

"Herald?" he asked. He'd never heard Kate use the term.

"That's the official title," she said. "Before one becomes a Warlord, one must be a Herald. That's what Hugh d'Ambray was before he became the Preceptor of the Iron Dogs."

Hugh d'Ambray. The name raised invisible hackles on his back.

He fought to keep the snarl out of his voice. "I didn't know Kate needed a Warlord."

"She doesn't. She has Curran. He is her Consort and her general."

His mind struggled for a few seconds. Those terms were usually flipped. To him, Curran was the Beast Lord, ex-Beast Lord now, and Kate was his Consort. That was the official title, and Kate had hated it. She would've never used it to refer to Curran. He knew where this was coming from, and he didn't like it.

"You've been talking to *him* again."

She didn't say anything, her gaze fixed on the street ahead.

Damn it. "Why the hell do you keep talking to him?"

"Because Roland teaches me things."

"What could he possibly teach you? How to be an immortal megalomaniac dickhead who kills his own kids? That's some great lesson."

"He teaches me magic." She glared at him.

"Stay away from him. He is dangerous."

She opened her eyes really wide and blinked at him. "Oh really? You think so? I had no idea."

He killed another growl. "You don't need to be talking to him. Nothing good will come from it."

"No, you are right. You are totally right. Let's not talk to the enemy we are all going to fight at some point." She shrugged her narrow shoulders. "Let's not try to figure out how he thinks or what weapons he might use. Honestly, Derek? You did all that spy stuff for Jim for years. I can't believe you."

"Believe it."

"I know!" She clapped her hands together. "Maybe we could all go into battle blindfolded."

He had an urge to pull her off her horse and shake her until some sense appeared in her brain.

"I can sew you a cute grey blindfold with some little scars on it—"

"He's a homicidal tyrant who's been alive for five thousand years!" he snarled.

"Six. Longer, probably, but he admits to six."

"Do you honestly think he's going to let you see anything he doesn't want you to see?"

"There are things he can't hide from me. Things that only I can see." She leaned forward. "He's teaching me, and that means I'm learning how he thinks. Someone has to talk to him, Derek. Kate isn't going to. That leaves me. I'm learning. I can make my own incantations now. I know how to build them and infuse them with power. That's something Kate doesn't know how to do."

"Incantations?" She was out of her mind. "Have you used one in an actual fight?"

"Not yet. It's dangerous."

"So he's teaching you something that may or may not work."

She glared at him. "It will work. I haven't used it yet, because it takes a crapload of magic. It's my last resort, and I haven't needed it."

"Kate doesn't need to incant. She uses power words." He had no idea how they worked. He knew only that they came from an ancient language and commanded the magic.

"That's what you think," Julie said.

"That is what I think. He's grooming you for something."

"Don't you think I know that?"

"Okay." He spun around and walked backward facing her. "Tell me one thing that you've learned that we don't know. One thing. Go."

"Okay. Do you know what he did to Hugh d'Ambray?"

"He exiled him. He should've killed him and saved us the trouble."

"No," Julie said quietly. "He purged him."

"What does that mean?"

"He took away his immortality. Roland was everything to Hugh. Father, mother, teacher. God. For sixty years, since he was a kid, Hugh did everything Roland asked exactly as he was told. All his life he tried to make Roland proud. And Roland cast him out. He stripped the gift of his magic from him and severed all magic ties between them. Hugh can't feel Roland anymore, Derek."

"And?"

"'When God shall remove all his presence from a man, that is hell itself,'" she quoted. "Hugh is in hell. He'll feel himself age slowly and know that eventually he's going to die."

"Good." He had no problem with that. Hugh had tried to kill Kate, he'd done his best to murder Curran, he'd almost started a war between the People and their vampires and the Pack, and he'd kidnapped Kate and nearly starved her to death, all in the name of trying to force her to meet with her father. The man's list of transgressions was a mile long, and Derek would happily take a payment in blood for every single one. If Hugh happened to step out of the shadows now, only one of them would leave this street.

"It would've been kinder to kill him," Julie said.

"Why are you so concerned about Hugh?"

"Think about it," she said, her voice sharp. "It will come to you."

He mulled it over. She was right. It came to him. "You are not Hugh."

"I am. I'm bound to Kate by the same ritual Roland used to bind Hugh."

"You're nothing like Hugh, and Kate is nothing like Roland."

Julie turned in the saddle and pointed to the northwest. "I can feel her. She's there."

He tried not to lie to her, so he said the first thing that popped into his head. "That's creepy."

"It is." She put a world into those two words.

"But creepy or not, you know Kate won't do what Roland is doing to Hugh. Roland doesn't love Hugh. She loves you. You're her child."

She sighed. "I know she loves me. That's why I'm worried. Derek, she still hasn't told me that I can't refuse her orders."

Alarm dashed down his spine. He hadn't realized she knew. "How long?"

"Roland told me months ago," she said.

"She hasn't told you because it's hard."

"I know," she said. "She tries not to order me around. She'll start to say some Mom thing and then stop, and you know she's rephrasing it in her head. It's kind of funny. Instead of 'Stop stealing Curran's beer out of the fridge and wash the dishes' it's all 'It would make me a lot happier if you stopped stealing Curran's beer' and 'It would be great if you did the dishes.' She probably thinks she's subtle about it. She isn't."

He didn't see anything funny about it. "What are you going to do?"

"It's not a problem now," she said.

"And if it becomes a problem?"

"I'll do something about it."

He didn't like the sound of that. "Still, you should stop talking to Roland."

She sat up straighter. "Will you stop bossing me around?"

"Stop doing stupid crap, and I'll stop."

Her eyes narrowed. "Eat my horse's ass."

Ugh. No thanks. "What, was Desandra at the house recently?"

"I don't need Desandra to teach me insults. And what the hell is it with all the comments about what I'm wearing? There's nothing wrong with these shorts."

"Don't you own any jeans?"

"I do."

"You should wear them."

"Why? Is the sight of my legs disturbing you, Derek?" She stopped Peanut and stuck her left leg out in front of him. "Is there something wrong with my legs?"

There was nothing wrong with her legs. They were pale and muscular, and men who should know better noticed them. He was not going to notice them for a list of reasons a mile long, starting with the fact that she was sixteen, and he was twenty. He sidestepped her leg. "The more protection between your skin and other people's claws, the better."

"I took down a werejackal. I'm not the one bleeding."

"I'm not bleeding."

"You were. And there is a rip in your hoodie where he got your shoulder."

He looked at her.

"Was I not supposed to mention it?" She put her hand to her chest. "So sorry, Sir Wolf."

"In a few hours I'll heal. You wouldn't. If you got cut up by a cat's claws, you would bleed unless we treated the wound. It would make you weak. Hours later you could reopen your wound if you turned the wrong way. Cats are filthy animals, and they carry all sorts of shit on their claws. You could die from an infection."

They made a right onto Birch Road. To the left the ruin of the mall spread out. During the mall's life, a narrow strip of lawn had ringed it, dotted by ornamental trees. Now the trees had grown, and thorny bushes sprouted between the trunks, forming nature's answer to a barbed wire fence and offering only glimpses of the mall beyond. Most of its buildings had long since crumbled into dust. The rains had washed it away, and an occasional sign was all that remained of the shopping center. He read the names—Burlington

Coat Factory, PayLess Shoe Store, Ross . . . They meant nothing to him.

"Did you share this cat view with Curran?" Julie asked. "Or are werelions slightly less filthy than other cats?"

He refused to take the bait. "A wound that's a minor inconvenience to me could be a death sentence for you."

Julie sighed. "Do you really think that if a wereleopard attacks me, jeans would stop him? Clothes don't have magic powers, Derek. They don't mystically protect you from three-inch claws, rapists, or murderers. If someone decides to hurt you, they will do so whether or not you have a thin layer of denim over your skin. Lighten up."

"It's better than nothing."

She narrowed her eyes, looking sly. He braced himself.

"I saw a picture of Hugh when he was your age," she said.

"Mhm."

"Hugh was a hottie."

His reaction must've shown on his face, because she threw her head back and laughed.

The road curved gently. They kept going around the bend, to the mouth of Orion Drive. Here no trees hid the mall, and the view was wide open. He stopped. Next to him Julie jumped off her horse, tied Peanut to a tree, and took a cloth backpack from among the saddlebags, hanging it over her left shoulder.

The parking lot unrolled before them, about fifteen hundred feet wide and probably two thousand feet long. Irregular holes pockmarked the asphalt, each filled with mud-colored opaque water. No way to tell how deep they were. A thin fog hung above the water, and in its translucent depths tiny green lights floated, their weak light witchy and eerie. In the center of it all, a spire of dark grey rock jutted out at a forty-degree angle, like a needle that had been carelessly thrust into the fabric of the parking lot. Rough and dark, twenty feet wide at the base and tapering to a narrow end, it rose about thirty feet above the parking lot. Pillar Rock. They would have to clear the parking lot to get to it. The three idiot shapeshifters had been told to meet their contact there.

Derek inhaled. He'd smelled swamp before; it smelled musky and green, of algae and fish and vegetation, like a heap of grass clippings that had been allowed to turn into compost, so new plants could grow from it. It smelled of life. This place smelled of mud and water, but no life. Instead a faint fetid smell of something foul, something rotting and repulsive, slithered its way to him.

Julie tensed, her hand on her tomahawk.

"What do you see?"

"Blue," she said.

Blue stood for human.

"Ugly, bleached-out blue, almost grey. This is a bad place."

He took a few steps back and sat on the curb. She moved into the scrub behind him. He heard the tomahawk bite wood. Leaves rustled, and she handed him a six-foot-long dry sapling. A walking stick. He took it and nodded. Good idea. She disappeared again, came back with a walking stick of her own, and sat next to him.

They waited quietly, watching, listening. Minutes dripped by. Mist curled above the dark water and shimmered in the moonlight. Julie didn't move.

A few years ago, when he was only eighteen, Jim, then Security Chief of the Pack, had put him in charge of a small group of twelve- and fifteen-year-olds who showed potential for covert work. Of all the things Derek tried to teach them, he found patience was the hardest. By now all of them would've scratched, or sighed, or made some noise. Julie simply waited. It was so easy with her.

They saw it at the same time: a brief flash of something pale as it moved within the deep blue shadow of the Spire. The hair on the back of his neck rose. Someone stared at them from those shadows. He couldn't see it clearly, but he felt the weight of its gaze, saturated with malice. It stabbed at him from the gloom. He pretended not to notice. Sooner or later it would get impatient.

The mist began to wane, thinning as if boiling off. It was luring them in.

"It will get foggy once we enter," he said quietly.

"Yes," Julie agreed.

There was no need to tell her to stay next to him. He knew she would.

"Look to the right, where the tree trunk splits," she murmured.

It took him a moment, but he finally saw it: the remnants of a small bundle of dried mistletoe hanging from the tree, tied with a leather cord. A small wooden medallion hung from the cord. A druid had been here, recognized it as a place of evil, and tried to contain it.

"Is the spell active?" he asked under his breath.

"No. It doesn't radiate magic. It's a linked ward and someone has broken it."

Magic and wards weren't his expertise, but he'd learned what he had to from Kate. A linked ward meant that identical wards had been placed all around the perimeter of the mall, forming a ring, each ward a link in a chain. If one link was severed, the chain broke, and the containment failed.

She shuddered. He felt her fear. Something about this place deeply creeped her out.

The mist thickened to the right, twisting. He pretended not to see the woman who stepped out of it. She was about twenty-eight or thirty, white and very pale. A ragged dress hung off her shoulders, once probably blue or green, but now faded to a dirty grey and damp. Her stomach bulged out—she looked either dangerously bloated or about seven months pregnant. She didn't smell pregnant. She wore no bra, and the fabric snagged on her erect nipples, tracing the contours of breasts. Her dishwater-blond hair fell to below her waist, framing her face like a curtain. It might have been a pretty face, he reflected, with sharp but delicate features, except her eyes were too hungry.

She walked up to the edge of the parking lot and stopped. "What are you doing here?"

"We're waiting to meet someone," Julie said.

"This is a dangerous place. Come with me. I have food."

Julie looked at him. He read hesitation in her eyes.

"She has food," he said, keeping his voice neutral.

"Then we should come."

"Come with me," the woman repeated, backing up. "Come."

If he were alone, it probably wouldn't have been food. It might have been sex. Or both.

He stepped into the parking lot, moving slowly, careful where he put his feet, tapping the stick in front of him. Julie followed closely. Out of the corner of his eye he saw the mist flood behind them, a milky impenetrable curtain.

"Come," the woman repeated, moving deeper into the lot, toward the spire.

He followed. The mist was swirling now, dense and thick. Ahead their guide stepped to the side and vanished.

He reached out with his left hand. Julie took it, her strong dry fingers grasping his. He reached forward with his stick and tapped like a blind man, listening for the splash. The stick landed into water. He tapped until he found solid pavement and they carefully skirted the hole, making their way toward Pillar Rock.

He kept tapping, guiding them between the holes. They passed another. Then another.

His stick landed into the water again. Something yanked it. He jerked back, pulling with all his strength. The mist burst, and the bloated woman lunged at him from the water. His mind registered the long claws protruding from hands with a scaly membrane between them and the enormous fish maw with the sharp pike teeth, but his body had already moved. He dodged, grasped her arm, and used her momentum to slide behind her, clenching her to him, her back to his chest, pinning her arms. Julie swung, her expression flat, and buried the three-inch spike of her tomahawk in the left part of the creature's chest. The scent of blood shot through him, like a jolt of electric current.

The woman flailed in his arms, trying to rake at him with her claws. He strained, keeping her still. He could snap her neck, but the fear still rolled from Julie. She needed this kill. Once she killed one, everything would fall into place.

Julie pried the tomahawk free and chopped at the woman's bulging stomach. It split like a water skin, and a half-decomposed human head rolled out. The sour stench drenched him and he nearly gagged.

The woman thrashed, kicking. Julie dodged, jerked a knife out of the sheath on her waist, and drove the six-inch blade into the woman's chest. The blade sank in with a scrape of metal against bone. The fish-woman screeched, her spine suddenly rigid, and sagged. The mist around them turned red and thinned, melting.

"Heart's on the right side," Julie said.

Claws grabbed him from behind and yanked him into the cold muddy water. He went under.

A body rushed at him through the coffee-colored water, long, pale green, clawed hands outstretched, a fish mouth on a human head gaping. A white light exploded in his head. The chain of will and restraint imposed by human part of him creaked, and he let himself off it. A knife was in his hand, and as she came at him, he locked his hand on the rough lip of that gaping toothed mouth and stabbed his knife into her side. He yanked the blade free and stabbed her again and again, driving the knife in with controlled frenzy. She clawed at him. He ignored the sharp flashes of pain and kept stabbing. Her side turned into raw butchered wound. She jerked now, trying desperately to break free, but there was no hiding from his knife or the white burning rage inside him.

Circles swam before his eyes. He realized his body was telling him it was running out of air. The creature floated limp, the right side of her chest a bloody hole. He thrust his hand into it, felt the deflated sack of the dead heart, and tore it out. Never leave things unfinished.

His chest hurt as if a red-hot band squeezed it. The first pangs of drowning panic scraped at his insides.

Darker shapes streaked toward him. Fish, he realized. Narrow and long, as long as his arm, with big mouths studded with teeth. They swarmed the body. He let go of the heart and kicked himself up.

He broke the surface and took a huge, lung-expanding breath. The air tasted so good.

Ten feet away, Julie spun like a dervish, her tomahawks slicing. She rammed the butt of her left axe under the third fish-woman's chin. The blow snapped the woman's chin up. Julie buried her right tomahawk in the creature's exposed chest. Blood gushed.

He pulled himself out of the hole.

The fish woman swung at Julie. The girl leaned back. The claws raked the air inches from her nose. She chopped at the woman's right side with her left tomahawk. Ribs cracked. The fish-creature dropped to her knees. Julie cleaved her neck. He heard the steel slice through the vertebrae. It sounded sweet.

The thin mist turned red again.

A shadow appeared behind Julie, rushing at her from the fog. He ran, picking up momentum, and leaped over Julie and the prone fish-woman. He rammed into the charging creature and tore into her. She broke like a rag doll in his hands, and he laughed. He snapped her arm, wrenching it out of the socket, her leg, her neck, her other arm, happy to finally release the rage he kept carefully pent up inside him.

A hand came to rest on his shoulder. "I get that this was terribly exciting, but she is dead. We killed everybody."

He snapped his teeth at her, playing, and broke the woman's forearm with a dry snap.

"De-rek," she said, turning his name into a song. "Come back to me."

Not yet.

"Look up," she whispered. "Look up!"

Fine. He raised his gaze. The moon looked back at him, cool and calm, glowing, serene. It washed over him, sinking deep into his soul, soothing the old scars and closing the new ones as it rolled through him. He felt the hot rush of fury receding, dropped the corpse, and stood up.

She handed him his knife. He must've dropped it during the jump. The parking lot spread before them, the mist a mere memory above the dark holes. He inhaled deeply and caught a trace of familiar blood.

"How bad?"

She lifted her shirt, exposing her side. A long scratch marked her ribs, swelling with angry red.

He opened his mouth.

The water exploded out of the holes, shooting up in filthy geysers. Julie swiped her backpack from the pavement. He grabbed her hand and sprinted to the pillar. They dashed, zigzagging between the water. The evil dark fish churned within the geysers. Dirty water chased them, flooding before them. He picked Julie up and *ran*. Pillar Rock loomed before them, and he leapt onto it. He ran all the way to the apex and lowered Julie next to him.

Below them, the parking lot became a lake. Long sinuous bodies writhed in the shallow water, feeding or panicking, he couldn't tell. He and Julie watched them quietly.

"Looks like we're going to be stuck here for a few minutes," she said, then gave him an odd look.

"Yes?"

She raised her backpack. "I have food."

He laughed.

No matter how hard Kate tried to remind him that he was first and foremost human, Derek knew himself to be separate. He was a shapeshifter. He never forgot it, and if he had, things like watching Julie wince as she smeared antibiotic ointment over her scratch reminded him. He could vaguely remember when he was human too, but that memory felt false, almost as if it had happened to someone else. Between it and his current reality lay things he didn't want to remember. If he reached down to stir them up, like old ghosts, he would recall them, but he didn't want to.

"Okay," she said.

He unrolled the long sticky strip of adhesive bandage and carefully placed it over her skin. The ointment would keep it from sticking to the wound itself.

Her ribs were no longer sticking out. He remembered when she was so skinny, he was worried she would walk into a lamppost by accident and break something.

She pulled her shirt back down and rummaged in her backpack. A plastic bag came out, with the second bag inside it filled with jerky, a bag of nuts and granola, and cheese. His mouth watered. He'd burned too many calories, and now he was ravenous.

She passed him the bags. Julie always had food. And she always wrapped it so it was hard to smell. It came from living on the street.

He snagged a long piece of jerky and chewed, reveling in the taste.

"You skipped the hunt again," she said, snagging a piece of cheese and a cracker.

The monthly hunts in the Wood, a big forest sprawling north of Atlanta, were a pleasant diversion for most shapeshifters. A way to blow off some steam. For him it was a necessity. He needed the wilderness. Without it the rage grew too fast. It would always be with him. Curran had told him there was no cure, and he was right. It was the price Derek paid for not turning loup like his father.

"Maybe," he said.

"What was so important?"

He shrugged. "Work."

She chewed her little sandwich, taking small bites out of it. She ate like a human too—a shapeshifter would've stuffed the whole thing in her mouth and would've been on her third sandwich by now. It was a test, he knew. She ate slowly to prove to herself that she could, that there was enough food and no need to rush because she wasn't starving.

"Lobasti," she said.

"Mhm?"

"The women. I think they were lobasti. Mermaids."

"Mermaids?" Somehow they didn't seem hot enough.

"Evil mermaids," she said. "I was so glad when that head rolled out. I thought I was fighting a pregnant woman. If I'm right, they only attack at night."

"Makes sense. The plan was to have those idiots recover the rock and bring it here. The mermaids would kill them, and then Caleb Adams would come in the morning, pick up the rock, and go home, his hands clean."

"That wereleopard doesn't know how lucky he is."

He won't feel lucky when he wakes up. He laughed quietly under his breath.

He was on his fourth piece of jerky. The burning fire in his stomach was subsiding. He would eat a big breakfast when they were done. Pancakes and sausage and bacon, and then he would sleep. . . .

"If we find out why the Iveses died over that rock, I'll make you all the bacon you want."

He startled.

Julie shrugged and bit her jerky. "I can always tell when you're thinking about food. You forget to be the Serious Wolf, and you get this dreamy look in your eyes. You know, most people would think you were thinking about a girl. They have no idea that her name is bacon."

"Dreamy look?"

"Mhm. Lighten up."

"I'm light enough."

He lay down on his back and looked at the moon, a strip of jerky between his teeth like a cigar. He slowly chewed on it.

"Thanks for the food."

"You're welcome. You used to joke more."

"You want jokes, talk to Ascanio." He yawned. "He's the funny one."

"Maybe you need a girlfriend."

"I left my pack. You know what that makes me?"

She sighed and recited, "A lone wolf?"

"Lone wolves don't have girlfriends." He put a little snarl into his voice. The injuries to his vocal cords didn't need much to make his voice into a low lupine growl. He'd used it more than once to make opponents rethink their battle plans and start looking for an exit. "We move around the city unseen, congealing out of the shadows when there's trouble and melting back into them so someone else can do the cleanup."

Julie laughed.

He grinned at her.

"Why is everything so grim all the time?" she asked.

For some people, the stars aligned and everything went right. For him everything went wrong, every time. When he wanted something, when he reached for it, life broke him, yet somehow he always survived.

All he'd wanted was to be a kid in the Smoky Mountains. His father had turned loup. He'd watched him torture and rape his mother and his sisters until he finally murdered the thing his father had become. The house had caught on fire. He'd been meant to die in that fire, but he'd survived.

When the Pack had found him, he smelled like a loup. The Code said he had to be killed on the spot, yet Curran had saved him. Again, he'd survived.

Then he'd wanted to be a shapeshifter, just a rank-and-file wolf, but by the time Curran finally coaxed him out of the deep dark mental well where he'd curled up and hid, it was too late. He was Curran's wolf, held to a higher standard. He was mocked. Normal avenues within the Pack were closed to him. The Renders wouldn't take him, so he went to work for Jim. His face was an asset. He could walk into a room and start a conversation with the prettiest girl and she would talk to him and smile, and her eyes would sparkle when he said something funny. He was good at gathering information, and he won respect, at first grudging, then well-deserved. He was good at being Jim's spy. They called him "the Face." He'd decided then that this was it. This was what he would do. This was his place.

He'd met Livie. She was beautiful, vulnerable, and gentle. She was trapped. She needed his help. She told him she loved him. He tried to help, but it ended with molten metal poured onto his face. He'd survived again, and went after her, putting everyone and everything at risk. In the end they broke her free, and the first free moment she had, she thanked him, said good-bye, and walked away to never return. He'd survived that, too.

The Face was gone. He still had the skills. He could throw witty one-liners, he could be charming without sounding smarmy, and he knew how to get people to open up and tell him things they normally kept to themselves. But his face was a barrier he couldn't overcome. Working for Jim had no longer been an option.

He'd tried other things after that. None of them felt right, until Curran and Kate separated from the Pack. He'd signed his separation contract half an hour after Curran signed his. He was the Grey Wolf in the city; the one who came and found you if you fucked up and hurt the wrong people. He helped those who needed it. He stood between those who were hurt and those who did the hurting. He removed threats, and soon his name alone would be enough of a deterrent. This new thing, it felt right. His face matched him now, matched how he felt and matched the role he chose. Jokes didn't.

There were other things he sometimes thought about. But those things were out of his reach. He got the point. Reaching for what he wanted would bring him pain. There was no need to share it with anyone. Explaining all this would be too long, and it would sound too melodramatic.

"Is there any cheese left?"

"Swiss?"

He wrinkled his nose. Swiss stank.

"Picky, picky, picky."

He liked cheese in general. Mozzarella was best. He snagged a piece of Swiss and held it on his tongue inside his mouth to see if the taste would make up for the smell. It didn't.

Julie leaned over. "The water is receding. Another half an hour and we can go."

A shadow dropped from the sky. He lunged forward, pulling Julie out of the way. A basketball-sized rock smashed into the pillar, a foot from her legs. He looked up in time to see a black bird shadow block out the moon and sickle-sized talons aimed for his face. He jumped to his right and up, punching into the bird from the side. It whipped around, huge wings beating, enormous yellow beak coming down on him like an axe. Talons tore at him in a flash of blinding pain. He locked his left hand on its throat, his right on its left leg, and pulled, trying to rip the huge raptor apart. It screeched, the high-pitched shriek nearly deafening him.

Julie screamed behind him.

He glanced over his shoulder. The rock was empty. Fear bit at him with icy teeth. He looked up and saw her dangling from a second huge bird twenty-five feet in the air.

He hurled the bird away from him, sinking all of his strength into the throw.

Julie fell.

Desperation propelled him into an insane leap. He caught her in midair, relief shooting through him as his arms locked around her, and then he twisted, trying to land on the pillar. The rock punched his feet. He landed hard, the shock reverberating through his legs, and fell backward, trying to keep them from hurtling over the edge. She landed on him. For a tiny moment they were face-to-face, and then she jumped off him. "The bag!"

He rolled to his feet. The two birds soared above them, melting into the night sky. He squinted and saw Julie's backpack hanging from the right bird's claws.

"They have the rock! And the sample! Damn it." Julie stomped on the pillar. "Damn it!"

She's alive, he told himself. Relax. She made it.

"They're flying northeast," he said. "That's the opposite way from the Warren and Adams' base. Can you see anything?"

She stood up and walked to the very edge of the rock and stood an inch from falling, looking into the city as if it were an endless indigo ocean and she was searching for that one sail at the horizon. She turned slowly and pointed. "There."

"Another glowing rock?"

She nodded.

Predictably, he couldn't see anything. "Where?"

She pointed northeast, in the exact direction the birds flew. "Maybe five, six miles."

He glanced behind them. "The Warren is there."

She turned and looked at the Warren. "Nothing there. If the birds belong to Adams, then he took what he had over there, or else the birds belong to someone else, and Adams knows how to hide his rock."

He searched the dark city. "And you haven't seen it before?"

"No."

"Let's say I'm Caleb. I want the shiny rock, but I don't like getting my hands dirty. I send some assholes to retrieve the two pieces of the rock. They get one from Luther, but they botch the other job, kill people, and cops are called. So I hire some idiot shapeshifters to go get the rock for me and bring it here. I break the linked ward guarding this place, so the fucked-up mermaids will eat the shapeshifters."

"Then, when it's daylight, the lobasti will hide and I'll come and get the rock," Julie said. "Easy."

"Except that if I were Caleb, I'd want to make sure that everything went according to the plan."

"You'd stay and watch." Julie's eyes narrowed. "You'd see us kill the lobasti and then hide on the pillar. You'd know we would be trapped up here for at least an hour. Plenty of time to make a new plan, summon some birds, and take the rock away from us. And then have them take it there?" She pointed to northeast. "Why?"

If Caleb watched, it was from afar, because Derek hadn't smelled him. He could've hidden in any one of the ruins around the place. Tracking him down was pointless—he'd left already, gone northeast with his own chunk of the magic rock. He would expect they would follow. He had all the time he needed to set a trap.

"Two possibilities. Either he has to do something with the rock over there, or he has figured out that you can see it. We keep interfering and screwing up his plans. He could be baiting a trap."

Derek wished he knew what the rock did.

Julie was looking into the distance, probably at the glowing rock, with a pinched expression on her face. She knew a lot more about witches than he did. Kate was related to one of the three witches on the Witch Oracle. Her name was Evdokia, and Julie had lessons with her every Tuesday.

"What do you know about Adams?" he asked.

"He's a warlock." She said the word as if it tasted bitter.

"A male witch." He knew that much. He also knew that Adams was feared. People didn't like mentioning his name.

"No." She shook her head. "He isn't a witch."

"What's the difference?"

"A witch strives for balance. For a witch, everything is connected. Everything is a tangle of binding thread; pull on one end too hard and you could make a knot nobody can untie. If you're sick, a witch will heal you, because plague is imbalance, but if you come to the same witch asking to give you another year of life through magic, he'll turn you down, because you're asking for something unnatural and there is always a price. The word *witch* comes from Old English *wicca*, an ancient word meaning a practitioner of magic. There are words similar to it, like *wigle* or *w h* in Old German, and they always mean things like divination, or holy, or knowing. Caleb Adams isn't a witch. He's a warlock. That word comes from Old English *wærloga*. It means traitor, liar, enemy. Oath-breaker. He cares only about his own gain, and he'll cut every thread he can to get what he wants.

That's why they cast him out of the coven. He broke his covenant. There's no limit to the fucked-up things he'll do to get his way. Evdokia hates him. Every time she mentions his name, she spits to the side."

A man like that would want the magic glowing rock for only one reason—power. Adams had already killed for it once. He would kill for it again, and if he obtained it, he would use it to keep killing. Derek thought of the Iveses. Of the bloodstains and blood scent, sickening because he knew the people it belonged to and because it called to him, threatening to wake up something he kept chained deep inside.

"There is only one thing to do," he said.

She looked at him, her face apprehensive.

"Let's go get the rock back," he told her.

Julie bared her teeth. She wasn't a shapeshifter, would never be one, but right now, under the light of the moon, she smiled like a wolf.

CHAPTER THREE

He jogged next to Peanut as Julie steered her down the overgrown street. They were moving northeast on Lawrenceville Highway, heading into Tucker. Since the city was now his territory, he took the time to learn about it. After the first Shift, when planes no longer worked and highway travel became dangerous, the industries looked to railroads for shipping. With buildings in Atlanta falling left and right, Tucker became the industrial hot spot for about fifteen years, growing fast until the newly built factories also decayed and fell. This was all ancient history, as far as he was concerned. Now Tucker stood abandoned, all but claimed by the wilderness, as the people pulled in to the heart of the city.

All around them dark ruins stabbed through the growth. A flock of school buses rusted, abandoned in some old parking lot. The remnants of a gas station, all but swallowed by dense kudzu, hunkered down to the right. Two owls sat on the remnants of the Exxon sign, waiting for some hint of movement. This would've been an ugly place without the green, Derek reflected. Sharp, rusted, trashed. The plants softened it, hiding the disfigured land underneath the happy leaves. Even the old power lines, dead for years, looked cheery, wrapped in vines and dripping small white flowers like garlands.

A creek had broken free of man-made restraints, flooding the road as it found an easy path down the paved highway. The water ran only a couple of inches deep, three at most, but he didn't like to get his feet wet, so he moved on the right side, where debris and soil deposited by the water formed a natural shore. Tiny fish darted in the clear stream. He smelled deer. A few moments later he saw them, too, drinking from a stream: a group of three does. Two were pregnant. They raised their heads, looked at him and Julie, and took off.

"Cute," Julie said.

She'd turned grim after they left Pillar Rock. He decided to yank her tail. "Delicious."

"Seriously?"

"Mhm. Later on I'll come back here and eat all of the deer babies. I'll be big and fat." No werewolf or human hunter would kill a pregnant doe or a doe with fawns. Do that often enough, and you risked your food supply. Then come winter, where would you be?

"If this is you trying to be funny, stop."

He grinned at her. "You wanted jokes."

"What kind of a joke is that?"

"Wolf kind."

"You really need a girlfriend."

Not that again.

"What about Celia?"

It took him a moment to figure out which Celia she was talking about. The Pack had four, and he interacted with three of them. It had to be the redheaded Celia. Before he separated from the Pack, she'd developed a persistent habit of thrusting herself into his daily routine. He could explain to her that every time Celia encountered him, he registered her noting his face with a calculated satisfaction.

She scrutinized his scars and judged him to be disfigured enough to be desperate. Celia craved power and safety. In her head he was perfect because he would stay, and be faithful, and he would let her hold the reins, since nobody else would have him. The single time they'd spoken in private confirmed it. She'd told him that unlike most women, she didn't mind the scars and that he didn't have to be alone. That she would have him, even if other women wouldn't. He'd stepped into her space then and held her stare. It was the dominating look of an alpha, and it communicated everything without words: He was neither weak nor desperate. She'd told him that if he touched her, she would scream, and she'd fled. He'd let her go. That had ended that.

"Celia is pretty."

"No." That was explanation enough.

"Then Lisa?"

He had to cut this short. Of all the topics she could've picked, this was the last conversation he wanted to have with her. He'd spent months learning to read people's emotions. He knew exactly what to say. He forced a smile. "You're a sweet kid, Jules, but don't worry so much. When you grow up, it will make more sense."

Her expression shut down, like someone had slammed a window into her closed. He'd drawn a line between a child and an adult and rubbed her nose in it. She would be mad at him for a while now. It was still better than discussing his love life.

The road took them deeper into Tucker. He smelled a skunk, raccoons, two roving bands of dogs, feral cats, and a big male bobcat that happily sprayed around. He didn't smell humans. Nobody had passed this way for quite some time. If Caleb Adams had taken the rock into Tucker, he hadn't come this way to do it or he'd had a giant bird carry him.

They traveled in silence for half an hour, when Julie turned off the road and steered her horse to the remains of a three-story building. She stood up in her saddle, grabbed the crumbling brickwork, and pulled herself up. He took a running start; jumped ten feet in the air; bounced from some rebar; ran across a narrow, half-rotten beam; and offered her his hand to pull her up. She gave him a look studded with broken glass. Right. Still mad.

"Come on," he said. "You're wasting time."

She ignored his hand and pulled herself over the edge onto the rotten remains of the third floor. He gave her space.

She raised her hand and pointed to an area in the distance. "There. It's in the center of that place."

He peered at it. Remains of some industrial complex, and a large one—at least two dozen big buildings, maybe more, some almost whole, others down to broken stretches of walls connecting to nothing. An accidental urban labyrinth. The soil around it was darker, the texture of it different, rougher somehow. Odd shapes rose among the ruins, some glowing with pale pink and blue. He couldn't quite make them out.

His instincts told him the place was unlike anything he'd seen before. And it felt bad. Pillar Rock made him wary, but this place felt worse. He didn't want to go in there, but most of all he didn't want her walking into it.

Like the dark soil around the ruins, Adams was a blight, a corruption that had already cost the Iveses their lives. The blight had to be purged. Curran had told him once, "Every time you see a problem and walk away from it, you set a new standard." The problem was right there, and letting Caleb

Adams butcher a family to get his hands on a magic rock wasn't a standard he cared to set. They would take care of it. It was time to cut the warlock's little power trip short.

He still didn't like it.

They circled the former industrial park, drawing a wide arc around it. Adams would expect them to come from the southwest. They approached from the north instead. The wind blew from the south, and he liked being upwind of his prey. They hid Peanut in the nearby ruins. With her backpack gone, Julie resorted to her backup bag, a small satchel she carried on her back.

From above, the walls looked shorter. Up close, some rose as high as ten feet. Giant mushrooms shaped like five-feet-high bay boletes, with pale blue caps the size of large umbrellas, clustered by the walls, their pores radiating a pale pink glow. The odd dark texture he'd seen from the top of the crumbling building turned out to be leaves—strange, purple-black plants no more than five inches tall, each a bunch of triangular leaves on short stalks. They blanketed the ground completely, spreading from the ruins like a puddle of spilled ink in an almost perfect circle, and they had to pick their way through thirty yards of them to get to the solid asphalt. He'd almost stepped on a rusty jagged spike sticking out of the dirt. Julie followed his footsteps, trusting his senses and another walking stick she picked up. Even so, they were barely ten yards in, and she'd stumbled once already.

The plants stank too. A heavy metallic scent that sat low, pooling near the ground. His nose would get used to it eventually, but for now he went scent-blind.

"Stop," Julie whispered.

A needle of alarm pierced him. Derek froze in midstep, his foot hovering above the ground, carefully stepped back, and raised his hand. She put the walking stick into it. He crouched and used the stick to push the leaves aside. A metal bear trap lay open among the leaves, the old-fashioned kind with a pressure plate and heavy-duty steel jaws armed with metal teeth. A chain stretched from the trap, snaking its way between the leaves. He glanced in that direction and saw an old, concrete power post. It had to be fastened around it. He'd seen these traps before. They weighed over fifty pounds, and the metal teeth would go straight through the bone.

"Adams did something," Julie whispered. "There is a blue stain of magic on the trap. It's faint and hard to see, but I've got it now. It's not witch magic; it's something else. Something really old. The whole field is seeded with them. Let me take the point."

They were sitting ducks out there. The faster they went through, the better.

He nodded.

A whine tore through the air, and a sharp spike of pain punched into his chest, exploding into white-hot, mind-numbing agony. Silver. The poison bloomed inside him, the agony ripping at him, spreading too fast. He didn't waste time glancing at the wooden shaft protruding from above his heart. Dropping flat would do no good. No cover.

The second arrow whined, only half a second behind the first. He thrust himself in front of Julie. It sank into his stomach. Silver exploded inside him. The detonation of hurt almost took him to his knees.

"Run!" she yelled at him.

If he tried to run back, they would be finished. Too much open ground behind them. They had to run forward, toward the bowman and to the shelter of the brick walls. If he pulled Julie behind him, she couldn't keep up. If he carried her in front of him, she would get shot. All of this flashed in his head in a torturous instant. He dropped, his back to her, grabbed her legs, shoved her on his back, and dashed forward to the ruins just as the third arrow sliced into the ground where he'd stood a moment ago. That was the only way the bulk of his body could shield her.

"Right!"

He turned right, sharp, almost falling, and sprinted. The pain ate at him from the inside, devouring his innards with burning fangs.

Another arrow whined and missed.

"Left! More left! Right! Straight!"

He shot out of the field of leaves into the shelter of a brick wall and smashed into it, unable to stop himself. The old bricks shuddered but held. He barely felt the impact. The fire inside him consumed all other pain. The silver poisoning spread as the virus that nourished his body died in record numbers. His legs shook, and he couldn't stop the trembling. The pain was spreading too fast. The arrows had been coated with silver powder.

He grasped the arrow shaft in his chest, focused on the brilliant spike of agony inside him, and pushed, forcing his dying muscles to obey. Julie's hand closed over his. He let go, and she pulled the arrow gently, carefully. His body fought him, trying to escape the pain. The world hovered on the edge of blackness. He snarled. The white spike vanished.

"Next," she said, grasping the second arrow, but he was already pushing with clenched teeth. It came free, but the suffering remained.

"Derek?" She looked into his eyes.

"Powder," he ground out.

Her face went white.

They had to move. They were too exposed here, and the shooter knew exactly where they'd fallen. He forced himself to his feet.

"Wait." She dug in her bag.

"No time." He pulled her up and leaned to glance around the wall. The night was empty. He moved, running quiet and fast. The silver burned its way through his veins. There was no time to expel it now. His body would either overcome it or die trying.

He ducked into the shadows, weaving his way through the maze of half-walls, aware of Julie next to him. They had to get to shelter, a higher ground, somewhere he could collapse for the few minutes he'd need to bleed himself. Somewhere hidden.

He smelled pungent smoke of burning herbs, too layered to parse into components. A thicker odor, dirty and hot, overlaid it. Some sort of animal, and more than one. Three, no four distinct scent trails, and below it all another scent. He took a whiff of it and recoiled. The scent was pure fear. It hit him deep in the gut, squeezing. He breathed in shallow quick breaths, trying to get a grip against the thought-killing primal panic.

Julie gasped. He turned. They'd come far enough to see around the corner of the larger wall. Beyond it, in a clearing, a circle smoldered on the ground, the scorched ground still smoking. Julie moved toward it before he could stop her. The revolting scent grew thicker. He followed, trying to shut down the terror snarling in his mind. The wall on their right ended, and Julie darted across the space. He cursed inwardly and followed.

She knelt by the circle, sheltered from view by the corner of the building. Charms and bundles of herbs hung from the bricks, each strung by a wet thread that smelled like flesh.

A wooden pole rose from the ground just outside the circle. Dead animals hung on it, each nailed to the wood with a long iron nail. A rat, a squirrel, a cat, and above them a wolf head smeared in fresh blood. Above the head, an arrow protruded from the wood. The arrowhead looked crude, almost ancient.

The wolf head stared at him with dead eyes, as if saying, *"Hey buddy. Don't fret. You and I are the same. There's no pain where you're going."*

Great. He had to bleed himself before the pain dragged him under or he started seeing things that weren't there.

"He summoned something," Julie whispered, her eyes wide. "He killed a wolf and summoned something very old."

He pointed at the herbs. "Are those wolf guts?"

"Yes."

A deep eerie howl rolled through the ruin. He jerked. *Run! Run now! He had to go. Dogs were coming and they would run him to ground. He was in the open, exposed, but he could outrun them if only he ran now, fast and hard, into the woods. . . .*

Julie grabbed his face with her fingers. "Look at me," she whispered, her words urgent and fast. "Look at me!"

He pushed her hands away, but she put them back, her fingers cold on his skin. She caught his gaze. He stared into her brown irises.

"Derek! He summoned a hunter. The animals on the pole are your prey, and you are the hunter's prey. This whole place is one giant magic trap, and it's trying to make you act in your assigned role. The hunter will sic his hounds, the wolf will run, and the hunter will chase and kill it. It's the way things were done for thousands of years, but you're not all wolf."

Another howl cut at him, like a sharp blade slicing at the nape of his neck. *Woods . . .*

Her hands held his face, her eyes two bottomless pools. "You're human. You're not all wolf. You don't have to run. You're human. Look at me. You're Derek. If you run now, you'll die."

If he ran, she couldn't keep up.

"You're human, Derek."

Her voice severed the welling panic. He felt reason returning slowly, slipping through pain and instinct. The things that howled would find them soon, and he was in no shape to fight. "We have to get to shelter."

She let him go. "If you run, the spell will lock on you, and you won't be able to break away. Don't run, Derek."

"I won't."

He turned around, fighting dizziness. A building—an old warehouse— loomed above the ruins to the right. It was obvious, but he didn't care. They needed shelter. He pointed to it. She nodded.

A sharp, triumphant howl sliced through the night. A hound was feet away, and it had just caught their scent.

To the left, the walls came together under a sharp angle, leaving only a narrow gap, half-choked by rubble. Anywhere else would put them into the open. He pointed to it.

Julie reached into her sack and pulled out a plastic bag of yellow powder. He took a deep breath and thrust his hoodie over his nose and mouth. She tossed the handful of wolfsbane into the air and backed toward him. They slipped into the gap. It terminated in a solid wall less than ten feet away. To the right, another wall. Above them, metal bars crossed. He could break them, but not without making noise. They were trapped in the twelve-by-twelve-feet space.

He went to ground. Julie lowered herself next to him. They peered through the gaps between broken bricks and dirt. Something grunted low and deep just behind the corner. Something big.

Derek lay completely still. The silver had eaten a hole in his chest and was trying to reach his heart.

Another grunt, harsh, loud. A beast ran into the open, huge, at least three hundred pounds and covered with long, coarse brown fur. In a bad light, he'd mistake it for a boar: It had the bulk, the shape, and the enormous boar jaws armed with tusks and massive teeth. But it had no hooves. Its legs terminated in clawed paws.

He had no idea if the wolfsbane would work on it.

The boar-hound snarled under its breath, sucking in the air. Small vicious eyes stared, unblinking. The creature took a step closer to the gap.

Next to him Julie held completely still. She couldn't take a hound. She'd need a spear. The tomahawks wouldn't do it. He had to fix himself fast or neither of them would get out alive.

Another step.

Another.

He reached for his knife.

The boar-hound inhaled, searching for their scent, and recoiled. It snorted, pawed at its nose, snarled, and squealed like a pig.

His ears caught the sound of heavy hoofbeats drawing near.

The boar-hound grunted, circling the smoldering ring, trying to get away from the wolfsbane.

A massive shaggy horse came into view, carrying a rider. Derek's view gave him a glimpse of a leather boot and a leg in brown pants. Derek dipped his head, trying to get a better look. The hunter wore leather. Big, at least six eight, larger, broader, probably stronger than a normal human.

A hooded cloak of wolf fur shielded his back. The invisible hackles between Derek's shoulders stood on end.

The hunter turned, showing his face. Around thirty, white, long brown hair. Hard. Weather-bitten. Light eyes. A long ragged scar crossing the nose bridge. Something with claws had marked him, but must've died before it finished the job. Derek bared his teeth. He'd make him choke on that fur.

A tall bow of wood and bone hung over the hunter's shoulder. The hunter raised an arm shielded by leather. A shriek tore through the night, and a bird dropped from the sky like a stone and landed on the arm. Ugly, bearded, big, with a vicious beak. Didn't look like any bird he'd ever seen.

The hunter studied the boar-hound, then raised his head and surveyed the area. His gaze passed over their shelter. He peered into the gap. Derek looked into his eyes. Magic rolled over him in a dark cold wave, dousing the agony of silver with ice, and he saw a long, frozen winter night under the moon. He felt the cold snow under his paws. He smelled his own blood, bright and hot, as it fell onto the snow, and heard the long, undulating howl of hungry hounds.

This is the way it always was. This is the way it had to be now. He had to run, run into the trees, before the arrows and hounds found him.

Nice try, asshole.

The urge to run was overwhelming now. It was taking all of his will to just stay still.

A moment dripped by. Derek waited. He was a wolf. He had all the patience in the world.

The hunter whistled softly through his teeth. The boar-hound shook its head and moved on. The hunter turned away, tossed the bird back into the night sky, and the massive horse resumed its steady walk.

They lay still for another three minutes before they quietly slipped out of the gap. Julie grabbed his hand, pointed to the pole, to herself, and up.

Lift me.

He grasped her legs and held her up. She plucked the arrow from the pole and they melted into the night.

The big building gaped open, its front wall gone, scattered in pieces on the ground. Half its roof was missing, but the back offered shelter. He was limping now, running slow even for a human.

"Almost there," Julie whispered.

He squeezed one last burst of movement from his body. He was shutting down.

"Almost there," she repeated.

He followed her across the dirty floor to the metal staircase leading up, up the stairs and to the far corner of the empty building. He sagged to the ground. She dropped beside him, yanked a small knife out of the sheath on her waist, and pulled his hoodie off. Her eyes went wide.

"It's over your neck."

He knew that already. The flesh over his neck and chest felt dead. When she touched it, he felt no pressure. The skin on his chest had turned duct-tape grey.

Cutting the chest wouldn't do it. The silver was still in his bloodstream and moving up. If it hit his brain, he would die. He had to expel it before it reached that far.

He snatched the knife out of her hands.

"Don't!" she gasped.

He slit his carotid artery. Blood sprayed in a black-and-red mist. He smelled the metallic stench of dead Lyc-V.

A howl, close, almost to them.

Julie whipped around and dashed down the stairs, her satchel in her hand.

Blood kept gushing in a heated flood, drenching his shoulder. Normally Lyc-V would've recognized the neck cut as fatal and sealed it nearly instantly, but the virus that granted his regeneration was dying in record numbers. He bled like a human, getting weaker with each beating of his heart. His hold on consciousness was slipping. His brain, starved of oxygen, was going to sleep like a dying fish. He hooked his claws into reality. A normal human would've been dead within seconds. If he could stay conscious, if his heart pumped enough silver-poisoned blood out for Lyc-V to recover, if the silver didn't reach his brain, he might survive.

Below, Julie drew a circle with white chalk around the stairs. A ward, a defensive spell. He doubted the chalk alone would hold the hounds or the hunter. She pulled the arrow from her bag and scratched a second line into the concrete floor, making the second ring inside the first chalk line.

The boar-hound appeared in the gap where the front wall used to be, silhouetted against the moonlight. He willed himself to move, but he could do nothing.

Julie yanked a small squeeze bottle out of her bag and poured a puddle in front of her, inside the circle.

Get up, he snarled at himself. *Get the hell up.*

The boar-hound let out a triumphant snarl of pure bloodlust.

Julie dropped into the circle on her knees. He saw a small flame of a match being struck. The puddle ignited.

The boar-hound charged. It came like a cannonball, snarling, giant maw open, tusks ready to rend.

Julie thrust something into the fire.

The hound covered the last ten feet.

Julie jerked the object out of the flame and held it up in front of her like a shield.

The boar-hound slid to a stop, its pig eyes fixed on the hot arrow in Julie's hand. The creature pushed forward and recoiled, as if striking an invisible wall.

He slumped in relief. The wound on his neck was closing. He was still alive. Now it was just a matter of time, and she had just bought them some.

The boar-hound howled. In the distance, three other voices answered.

He wasn't sure how much time had passed: seconds, minutes. But the wind had changed, and he smelled the second hound before he heard it charge its way into the building and slide to a stop before Julie's circle. Third and fourth followed. He heard the bird, saw it as it flew over him, circling, and then he heard the hunter's horse.

He heard the rough sound of metal striking stone. She was chopping at the arrowhead with her tomahawk.

The pain in Derek's neck had ebbed. The edges of the gray skin shrank, turning pink, not fast enough but it would have to do. She had done her part. It was time for him to do his.

In the darkness of the second floor, he slid his shoes off, then his pants.

The horse clopped its way into the building.

"You cannot break it," a deep male voice said.

He looked down. The hunter stopped his horse midway down the floor. The four boar-hounds lined up between him and Julie.

Here you are, asshole.

"The arrowhead's stone. This is stainless steel." She sounded determined. "I'll shatter it."

Derek rose quietly in the shadows.

"That is my first arrow. The arrow is eternal and so am I. As long as there are humans and their prey, I will exist."

"Go fuck yourself." She smashed the tomahawk into the arrow.

Now. The change dashed through him, the brief pain welcome and sweet. His muscles tore and grew again, his bones lengthened, his fur sprouted, and suddenly he was whole again, stronger, faster, seven feet tall, a meld of beast and man. The burn of silver was still there, but now just a razor-sharp reminder of the pain and the need to kill its source. He smelled blood. His three-inch claws itched. He heard eight hearts beating: five animal, one bird, and two human. He wanted to taste the hot, salty rush of blood pounding through their veins, to open them and feel them struggle in the grip of his teeth.

The wild within him roared. The thing that nearly turned him loup—the one he kept at bay with monthly trips to the woods, with meditation, with exertion, with running until his legs could no longer carry him—that thing broke free and it was hungry.

"Choose a side," the hunter said.

Her voice rang, her words defiant. "I choose the Wolf."

"Then you die." The hunter pulled the bow off his shoulders.

Not today. Derek leaped over the iron rail. He landed among the hounds and opened two throats, tusk to tusk, before they realized he was there. Blood gushed—glorious, hot blood, straight from the heart. The wild sang within him. The third beast tried to gore him, but he hurled it aside like a rag doll. It hit the wall with a loud thud, whimpered as it slid to the ground, and lay still.

An arrow whistled through the air. He grasped the fourth beast by its neck and jerked it up, holding the struggling animal like a shield. Arrows thudded into it—one, two, three—and sank deep. He hurled the creature at its master. The horse reared, screaming. The hound met the hunter's fist and fell, knocked aside. It scrambled to its feet and ran to Derek, limping. The remaining hounds, two slashed and bleeding and one favoring its front leg, rushed him. He dodged the first, letting it rush past him, and landed on its neck and bit. His teeth closed around the spinal column and crushed the cartilage. He tore a mouthful of flesh and bone and let go. A tusk dug into his hip. He snarled at the pain and punched the creature's thick skull. It shuddered and he punched again, driving his fist in with all his wild strength. The bone broke. Brain wet his fur. The last hound attacked, unsteady on its feet. The wild roared inside him, so loud he could hear nothing else. He carved the hound's throat into pieces.

An arrow pierced his thigh. He ripped it out, slashing the wound open before the silver could spread.

The last beast fell. The bird swooped down at him. He snatched the raptor out of the air and tore off its head. Only the man was left. He walked to the hunter. There was no need to rush.

The hunter drew his bow and fired. Derek knocked the arrow aside. Another arrow. He dodged. It grazed his thigh. The burn of silver spurred him on. Derek leaped and took his opponent off the horse with a swipe of his paw. The big human rolled to his feet, two blades in his hands. They were almost the same height: the hunter nine inches over six feet tall, and he fully seven feet in his warrior shape.

Derek licked his fangs. Delicious blood coated his tongue and dripped from his mouth, but he was still hungry.

The hunter became a whirlwind of blades. He sliced and stabbed and cut fast, very fast. Derek blocked, stepped inside his guard, and kicked him in the chest. The hunter flew backward, rolled to his feet again, and charged.

They collided. A blade pierced Derek's chest, sliding neatly between his ribs, almost nicking his heart. The pain tore at his insides. He buried his claws in the hunter's gut and tore a handful of intestines out. The hunter twisted the sword, trying to carve his way to Derek's heart. Derek stepped back, pulling himself off the blade, and the hunter chopped at his right arm with the other sword. He took that cut, because he had no choice—it nearly cut through the bone—and raked his claws across the hunter's face. Blood poured into the hunter's eyes. The big human lunged, his right sword striking. Derek moved to the left, letting the blade whistle past, locked his right arm on the hunter's wrist and smashed the heel of his left hand into the man's elbow. The joint snapped, breaking. He jerked the blade from the hunter's suddenly limp fingers and rammed it into the hunter's mouth.

It was a good sword, sharp and solid. It made a lovely sound as it split the hunter's mouth, then his throat on its way down. The hunter's heart fluttered like a dying bird, then stopped.

Derek raised his head to the sky. Above him the moon watched through the massive gap in the roof. He opened his bloody jaws and sang. The high-pitched howl rose up, riding on the moonlight, rolling through the night, and all who heard it would know he had made his kill.

He shook the corpse, hoping for more fight, then took the dead man's head into his mouth, but the hunter didn't move. His heart was still. He tossed the dead hunter aside.

There had to be something left to kill. There was still one heart beating.

He turned and saw her sitting in a circle. She looked . . . *good.*

He walked to the circle. She didn't move. She just watched him with pretty brown eyes.

He ran headfirst into a wall. He couldn't see it, but it was there. He looked down and noticed a white chalk line between him and her. Magic.

He circled the ward, probing it with his claws. The invisible wall held all the way around. He stopped in front of her and crouched, so they were level. His voice was an inhuman, ragged snarl. "Let me in."

"I don't think that would be a good idea."

"Let me in."

"Maybe in a little while," she said. "Once you cool off."

"I'm all cooled off." He wanted into that circle.

"In a little bit."

He backed away and ran full speed at the circle. The wall held.

"You really can't skip the hunt," she told him.

It took another four tries before he decided he couldn't break through the wall. He kicked the corpses for a while, but they didn't put up a fight and the horse had run off. He thought of tracking it down, but he would have to leave her and he didn't want to. He finally settled for stretching out by the circle and looking at the moon.

It soothed him until his breath evened out. Slowly the rational thought returned. His body hurt in too many places. He wished he could fall asleep, but if he let himself go now, he would sleep like the dead for several hours while his body healed the damage. He couldn't change shape either. Most shapeshifters could deal with one or two changes in a day and then it was nap time, whether you liked it or not. He was stronger than most, but he didn't want to tempt the fates. He'd spent so much energy fighting the silver, a change could shut him down for good, and he didn't have that luxury.

Caleb Adams was still out there.

The deep purple of the night sky was slowly fading to lighter blue. The sunrise was coming.

The wild had gotten away from him. It was always like this—he remembered what he did only after he had done it. It always felt right while he was doing it. Sometimes he regretted it, although mostly he didn't. He did today.

"Derek!" she sounded alarmed.

He sat up.

"The rock is moving." She pointed right. "He's taking it somewhere!"

He shook himself. "Come on."

She squinted at him.

"I'm cooled off," he told her.

She reached over, rubbed the chalk line, and stepped out. Her scent washed over him.

"Which way?" he asked.

"East," she said. "No, wait, southeast. He's going back exactly the way we came."

"Sorry I scared you," he said as they left the building.

She rolled her eyes. "You're not that scary."

Relief washed through him. He bared his fangs at her, pretending to snarl.

"Ew. Drool. Nothing you do scares me, Derek. Deal with it."

"I'll have to try harder then."

"You do that."

Chapter Four

The sky above Pillar Rock was a pretty blue, with thin trails of clouds stretching from the east. The muddy water of the holes stole the color, and for the moment, turned blue and shiny, like cobalt glass. The pillar jutted among the myriad of puddles, reaching toward the sky, and on its very tip, three chunks of glowing rock lay together, forming a single glowing stone. It was almost beautiful, Derek reflected, except for Caleb Adams, who stood between them and the pillar. He'd caught Adams' scent the moment they left the ruins. The warlock made no attempts to mask the trail. A child could've followed it.

He was in his forties, average height, but above average build, if his broad shoulders and stance were anything to go by. His black robe, tattered and tied with a length of rope, probably hid the build of a weightlifter.

His face was perfectly ordinary: short, dark blond hair; short beard; dark eyes under sloping eyebrows. His face had a ruddy tint, just short of a sunburn, the kind pale-skinned people got when they were forced to spend time outdoors. Clever, Derek decided. If Adams walked into a bar and ordered a beer, Derek wouldn't pay him a second glance.

"I have to know," Adams said. "What the hell is it? Who hired you? Why are you following me all around the damn city? I just can't shake you two off."

Derek unhinged his monster jaws. "Your people killed the Iveses."

"So that's it?" Adams frowned.

"Kids," Julie said. "They killed the kids, too. You don't get the rock. You don't get the power. You get to answer for the family."

"This is what comes from sending idiots to do a job." Adams sighed. "There are ten rules to delegation. The first one is pick the right people. Clearly, I picked the wrong people."

Either he was obsessed with middle management or he was stalling. He had some sort of plan. Derek glanced at Julie. She looked back at him, her face unreadable. If she had seen any magic, she would've shook her head or nodded or given him some sign.

"You win." Caleb raised his hands, backing off to the left. "I know who the two of you are. You're the Grey Wolf, and you're Kate Daniels' little witchling. I've seen the two of you around. I thought the Hunter would take of the two of you, so I could do my thing, but clearly he didn't. I give up. There's the rock; go and get it."

Neither of them moved.

"You do know what it does?" Caleb smiled. "The glowing star, falling from heavens at sunset on the last night of spring? A nightingale wasn't singing—we don't have them here—but a mockingbird was. It's close enough. Normally they don't break like that, but magic is still weak in the world. You should know this, little witchling. This is one all Slavs fear. Or did Evdokia not teach you yet?"

"Derek!" Julie cried out. "Run!"

The first ray of the rising sun broke free from the horizon. The glowing rock shone with brilliant, cold light, fusing into whole. The light shot up and coalesced into a woman.

He took a sharp breath.

She was beautiful. Her skin was flawless, her hair like gold, her eyes silver like starlight. She stood naked on the rock. He stared at her breasts, the rounded curves of her hips, the pale triangle of golden curls between her legs . . . So soft, so golden . . . He wanted to put his hands on her.

Her magic washed over him, and his body reshaped itself on its own, trying to match her humanity with his own. He went hard, and when she opened her mouth, her red lips like ripe fruit, and called him to her, his body wanted to obey.

Her voice was the most beautiful sound he'd ever heard. *"Beloved . . . Come to me . . ."*

Images flickered in his mind. He saw himself over her, felt himself in her, saw her skin blush as her body clenched around him. . . . Her magic was too strong. He was tired and hurt, and the forced change drained him. He couldn't fight it. He had to go to her. That was the best way. The right way.

"Derek!" Julie grabbed his arm. "No!"

He shrugged her off. He had to get to the woman. Fighting the flood of magic was pointless. It would only exhaust him more, and he was already weak.

"Derek!"

He shoved her back. She fell and he marched to the pillar.

"He's lost," Adams mocked. "He's young and single. He can't resist a letavitsa. That right there is unmatched power. A single one can empty a city of every man in it."

"Derek!"

He heard her trying to run after him and, out of the corner of his eye, saw Adams pull a knife out and step into her path.

"You'll die next," Julie snarled.

"I took measures. I have protection. He doesn't. The fallen star will feed on him and drain him dry. Now it's just you and me."

"Come closer. . . . Tell me you love me. Give yourself to me."

He let the magic pull him forward. It was too strong to fight. He had to give himself to her. He was almost to the Pillar Rock.

Adams raised his hand. Foul magic spread from him, like dark ink. "Evdokia will just love this."

"What the hell do you want with a letavitsa anyway?"

"Funny thing about gangs," Caleb said. "Ninety percent of members are male between the ages of fifteen and twenty-five. Rabid with hormones and unlikely to form lasting attachments. A man would have to be willing to die for a woman to fight off the letavitsa's magic. That kind of devotion is rare. Tomorrow night I'll walk with her through the Warren, and that will be the end of my turf war."

Derek jumped onto the pillar and began walking toward her. She waited, golden, warm, ready, her hair floating around her, her silver eyes glowing. . . . He could see Julie and Adams below them among the puddles.

"I'm the Herald," Julie said. Her voice had an odd cadence. "I serve the Guardian of the City."

"Well, your Guardian isn't here." The dark magic around Adams coalesced. Black serpentine shapes slid within it, stretching from him, each tipped with a skeletal dragon head armed with needle-sharp teeth.

"Her blood is my blood. Her power is my power."

Adams halted. "Cute. Are you incanting, little one?"

"Look into my eyes and despair. For I'm Punishment, and you cannot escape me."

The black smoke serpents streaked to her, their skeletal mouths opening wide, their smoke bodies billowing with black.

Magic punched from her, sweeping the smoke serpents aside. For a fraction of a second Adams froze, his face shocked.

Julie opened her mouth. *"Karsaran."* The sound rocked her. She dropped to her knees.

An unseen power jerked Adams off his feet. His body froze, rigid. A sharp short tremor shook him with a loud sickening snap, as if every bone in the warlock's body had broken. The body fell onto the ground.

Julie straightened, wiped the blood from her nose with the back of her hand, pulled out her tomahawk, and walked toward Adams, her mouth set in a hard line.

He saw Adams' mouth gaping.

"He'll still die," the warlock squeezed out.

"Come, beloved. . . . Give me your love. I will make you whole."

"I'm coming," he said. He was almost to her, to that celestial pliant body, so soft, so eager for him. Ready. Willing.

Julie raised her tomahawk and chopped down.

The golden woman opened her arms. She was so beautiful, he wanted to weep. He wanted that body. To claim it, to feel her flesh under his fingers. . . . She smiled at him, and visions of her mouth swirled in his mind. He didn't care that it was filled with sharp serrated teeth. He wanted to taste those red lips. The need was there, but it wasn't coming from him.

She reached out and stroked his face with her fingertips. Her silver eyes shone. Her voice came in a shocked whisper. *"You belong to someone else."*

"Yes." His body tore with the last of its strength. The wolf spilled out, and he shoved his clawed hand into her chest. His claws punctured her heart. He tore it out.

She screamed, shocked, her shark teeth bared. Her body burst into ash. For a moment, it held together, and then the wind swept it off the rock into the city.

He was so tired, he didn't feel himself falling. He didn't hear Julie scream.

When he opened his eyes, the sky was the soothing night blue again. A thin blanket covered him. He was warm and aching in a dozen places, the last granules of silver burning like dying coals inside him as his body slowly pushed them to the surface of his skin. His head rested on something that smelled like horse—probably a saddlebag. Around him, the city stretched, the rare golden lights of electric lamps glowing weakly from a distance. He was still on Pillar Rock.

He caught Julie's scent. It swirled around him and he savored it. No blood. She wasn't injured. They'd made it through.

"Finally," Julie said.

He sat up, wrapping the blanket around him like a robe. She smiled at him.

"How long was I out?"

"The whole day."

She had stayed with him. She hadn't left and called for pickup; she'd just stayed here, where he'd fallen, and watched over him.

Julie dug in the bag. "I grabbed some food from the food cart passing by. It's not deer babies, but you'll just have to suffer through it."

He reached out and touched her hand.

She paused and looked at him, her eyes bottomless.

"Thank you."

"For what?"

73

"For staying with me."

"You're welcome, Wolf," she said quietly.

He realized then that she would've sat by him as long as it took and that he was still holding her hand. He made himself let go.

She looked away and pulled smoked venison and a jug of iced tea out of the bag. "Eat. You're probably starving."

"In a minute," he said. "The moon is almost up."

She put the bag down and lowered herself next to him. They sat quietly on Pillar Rock, side by side, almost touching and happy to be alive, and watched the moonrise.

Epilogue

"**A**nything exciting happen while we were gone?" Kate cut the freshly baked bread in the kitchen.

"No." That was one good thing about living on the street, Julie reflected. You learned to lie while your eyes shone with sincerity. "And you didn't even mention my awesome timing. You came through the door, and there was bread already baked for you."

Behind Kate, Curran glanced at her. He'd called Derek about the Iveses, so he knew, but Kate clearly didn't. They would have to tell her, but not tonight. Tonight she was tired and hungry, and the look on her face when she came downstairs after she took a shower to wash all the blood off was too relaxed. Julie smiled at Curran. *It will wait.*

"Thank you for the bread. You sure nothing happened?" Kate arched one eyebrow.

Julie remembered finishing off Adams, seeing Derek fall as he turned human again, and then running too fast up Pillar Rock. She'd dropped to her knees and put her head on his chest, and when she'd heard the strong, even heartbeat, she'd cried and then kissed his lips gently, because he was asleep and he would never know. He'd scared her so much.

Stupid wolf. Her stupid, stupid wolf.

Kate wouldn't understand, and she didn't need to know. "Nothing happened."

"That's odd. We dropped by the office on the way home and there is a check from Luther in the payment box. A large check."

"I sold him a magic arrow," she said. "It was very old. The arrowhead was stone. Ask him if you don't believe me."

Kate squinted at her.

It was time to beat a hasty retreat before more questions came. Julie headed for the kitchen door.

"Where are you going?"

"I'm going to give Peanut her nightly carrot."

She stepped out and shut the door behind her. Escape accomplished.

The air was comfortably cool. An early evening had fallen, and the sky was a deep purple studded with stars. They winked at her as she walked.

Keep winking. As long as you stay up there, we won't have a problem.

She opened the stable door, grabbed a carrot from the treat bag hanging from a hook, and walked to Peanut's stall. The horse reached for the treat, and the soft velvety lips brushed her palm.

A presence appeared behind her. She felt it—a knot of arcane power, burning from within, like standing with her back to a stove, if heat were magic. That's what old nuclear reactors must've been like. An unimaginable potential for destruction concentrated in one small space.

"You finally used your power," the immortal wizard said.

She didn't turn around. "Yes."

"How did it feel, Herald?"

The memory of power ripping from her in a torrent surfaced in her mind, followed by a spike of pain as she said the power word after her incantation had paved the way. She heard the sound of Adams' bones breaking and patted Peanut's nose.

"How did it feel?"

The Herald of Atlanta smiled. "It felt good."

ACKNOWLEDGMENTS

Many people have helped make this novella a reality. With gratitude we would like to thank

Nancy Yost, our agent, whom we continue to drive nuts and who was on board with this project even though it came out of the left field;

Deanna Hoak for the wonderful copyedit;

Doris Mantair for the amazing cover;

Shannon Daigle, Kristi DeCourcy, Kate Scheu, Toni Grasso, Robin L. Snyder, Chris Schanck, Jeanne L.D. Osnas, Hagar Michaeli, Julie Heckert, Hasna Saadani, Mindi Mymudes, Jessica Haluska, Ying Dallimore, Helen Gordon, and others for beta reading the manuscript;

Natanya Wheeler, for the formatting and upload and troubleshooting all things ebook;

Sarah Younger, for her work on the print edition;

Adrienne Rosado for the audio;

And finally, thank you to the readers, who requested this novella until we wrote it. We hope you like it.

Discover More by Ilona Andrews

KATE DANIELS Series in Order
A Questionable Client (prequel short story)
Magic Bites
Magic Burns
Magic Strikes
Magic Mourns (Raphael and Andrea novella)
Magic Bleeds
Magic Dreams (Jim and Dali novella)
Magic Slays
Gunmetal Magic (and Magic Gifts) – Andrea's
book – Kate Daniels World #1
Magic Rises
Magic Breaks
Magic Steals (Second Jim and Dali novella)
Magic Shifts
Retribution Clause (Set in Kate's world, but in
Philadelphia with Saiman's cousin. Set com-
pletely outside of Kate's storyline.)
Magic Tests (Julie's short story, happens after Magic Slays)

THE EDGE Series
On the Edge
Bayou Moon
Fate's Edge
Steel's Edge

HIDDEN LEGACY Series
Burn for Me
White Hot

INNKEEPER CHRONICLES Series
Clean Sweep
Sweep in Peace

About the Author

Ilona Andrews is the pseudonym for a husband-and-wife writing team. Ilona is a native-born Russian and Gordon is a former communications sergeant in the U.S. Army. Contrary to popular belief, Gordon was never an intelligence officer with a license to kill, and Ilona was never the mysterious Russian spy who seduced him. They met in college, in English Composition 101, where Ilona got a better grade. (Gordon is still sore about that.)

Gordon and Ilona currently reside in Texas with their two children, and many dogs and cats. They have co-authored two series, the bestselling urban fantasy of *Kate Daniels* and romantic urban fantasy of *The Edge*.

Visit Ilona Andrew's website, www.ilona-andrews.com, for the latest news, freebies, and other fun things.

CPSIA information can be obtained
at www.ICGtesting.com
Printed in the USA
LVOW03s0421240917
549694LV00001B/3/P